Lineberger Memorial
Library
Lutheran Theological Southern Seminary Columbia, S. C.

TENTH AVENUE COWBOY

Written by **Linda Oatman High** *Illustrated by* **Bill Farnsworth**

Eerdmans Books for Young Readers
Grand Rapids, Michigan Cambridge, U.K.

Published in 2008 by Eerdmans Books for Young Readers
an imprint of Wm. B. Eerdmans Publishing Co.

William B. Eerdmans Publishing Co.
2140 Oak Industrial Dr NE, Grand Rapids, Michigan 49505
P.O. Box 163, Cambridge CB3 9PU U.K.

www.eerdmans.com/youngreaders

Manufactured in China

14 13 12 11 10 09 08   8 7 6 5 4 3 2 1

Library of Congress Cataloging-in-Publication Data

High, Linda Oatman.
Tenth Avenue cowboy / written by Linda Oatman High ; illustrated by Bill Farnsworth.
p. cm.
Summary: In 1910, when his family moves to New York City from their ranch out West, Ben misses the cowboys and the prairies that they left behind, but after he learns that there are cowboys in the city who race along the railroad tracks and warn people of approaching trains, he begins to feel more at home.
ISBN 978-0-8028-5330-1 (alk. paper)
[1. City and town life — New York (State) — New York — Fiction. 2. Cowboys — Fiction. 3. Railroad trains —Fiction. 4. New York (N.Y.) — History — 1898–1951— Fiction.] I. Farnsworth, Bill, ill. II. Title.
PZ7.H543968Te 2008
[E] — dc22
2007028190

Illustrations created with oils on canvas
Display type set in AtlanticInline.
Text type set in ITC Caslon No. 224 BT

For Janet. My gratitude for friendship that never ends and for the suggestion that
we go visit Bill in Venice that October day. Blue sky, yellow sun, red convertible Jag . . . and now a book.
You are still Little But Mighty, my longtime friend.
And for my parents, who tolerated the cowgirl in me. Thanks for the horses.

— *L. O. H.*

For Chuck.

— *B. F.*

It was 1910
when Ben and his parents
left their ranch in the West
and took the train
to New York City,
where they'd heard
the work and the pay were the best.

Papa got a job in the Hell's Kitchen
section of New York,
working in a blacksmith shop.

Ben didn't like Hell's Kitchen.
He didn't like the city smells
or the crowded sounds
or the brownstone tenement apartment.

The tough boys of the neighborhood
made fun of Ben's western accent,
and they called him a sissy.
Some of the girls bullied him, too,
because Ben was so quiet.
Ben wished that he fit in.
He wished for a friend.

Ben missed his home,
and the great plains of the West.
He missed the bridges
and rivers and the grass prairies.
But most of all,
Ben missed the cowboys.

Ben dreamed of being a cowboy.
He wanted to wear chaps and hats,
bandanas and spurs.
He longed to ride high and gallant
on a galloping horse.

Ben no longer had a horse, though.
His family had left
their horses at the ranch
when they moved to New York City.

But Ben watched the horses
in the city
and in the blacksmith shop.
He studied the horses
that pulled ice wagons
and the horses
hitched to fancy carriages.

Then one day
Ben heard about the
Tenth Avenue Cowboys,
whose job was to ride before the train
and warn people of its approach.

Ben couldn't believe it:
there were cowboys
in the city!

Many times day or night,
a horse would charge down
Tenth Avenue, where railroad tracks
were set into the cobblestones
of the city street.

Hooves sparking
and mane whipping in the wind,
the horse would gallop
with a Tenth Avenue Cowboy
riding fearless and tall in the saddle.

In a city canyon
with brownstone buildings for mountains,
the city cowboys rode,
carrying flags in the daytime
and red lanterns at night.

One day, a Tenth Avenue Cowboy
brought his horse
into Papa's shop
for new shoes.

The cowboy, Johnny,
told Ben about the Pebble Yard
on Tenth Avenue and 30th Street,
where the cowboys put up their feet,
waiting for the train whistles to blow.

Johnny told Ben
about the stable on 37th Street,
where the cowboys
took the horses at the end of their rides.

Johnny invited Ben
to visit the horses with him.

After that, Ben was at the stable
every day, bringing treats for the horses.
He adored them all.

Johnny took Ben
to the Pebble Yard one afternoon.
The cowboys were
playing cards to pass the time.
Ben asked him
if he could ride a horse.

Johnny let Ben
try on his cowboy hat.
It was much too large,
but Ben loved the feel
of the soft brim against his ears.

“Time for a ride,”
Johnny said when it was time
for his shift to begin.

Sitting high in the saddle,
Ben felt as if he were on top of the world.

Ben took a deep breath.
He whooped
as the horse galloped
mightily down Tenth Avenue.

The train hooted
from far down the tracks,
and the horse's back rippled.

Holding on with all his might,
Ben rode fast into a city canyon
with brownstone buildings
for mountains.

People watched in wonder
as the horses thundered by,
galloping fast, bolting past
the clamoring locomotive.

Ben glanced at the children,
and they were cheering for him,
amazed that he was riding
with a Tenth Avenue Cowboy.

Ben closed his eyes for a moment,
and he saw the great plains
of the West: bridges and rivers
and prairies of grass.

He opened his eyes, and there were
the usual city sights of
tenements and factories
and crowded city streets.

Ben heard Johnny's voice above the noise,
"Soon you'll be a Tenth Avenue Cowboy too."

Then magic happened:
Ben's white horse
seemed to glow in the moonlight,
and the city felt warm and familiar.
Hell's Kitchen looked
like heaven to Ben.

Ten years later,
Johnny looked about the same,
except for a few more lines on his face.
But Ben had grown up,
and the city was now his home.

Author's Note:

The Tenth Avenue Cowboys were legendary figures in Hell's Kitchen, where they rode their horses to warn of the approaching trains until the early 1930s. The Cowboys gave city youngsters a thrill of the West, and the children of Hell's Kitchen admired those who rode high and gallant on the galloping horses. Many children longed to be a cowboy themselves one day, and some of them succeeded.

— *Linda Oatman High*

Glossary:

Hell's Kitchen: a poor area of New York City, known in the 1900s for violence and general disorder

Brownstone tenement building: an apartment building used to house large numbers of low-income families

Gallant: splendid, brave

Chaps: protective leather pants that cowboys wear over trousers

Blacksmith: a person who makes objects out of iron or steel, like horseshoes

Cobblestone: the type of stone frequently used in the pavement of early streets

Locomotive: railway train